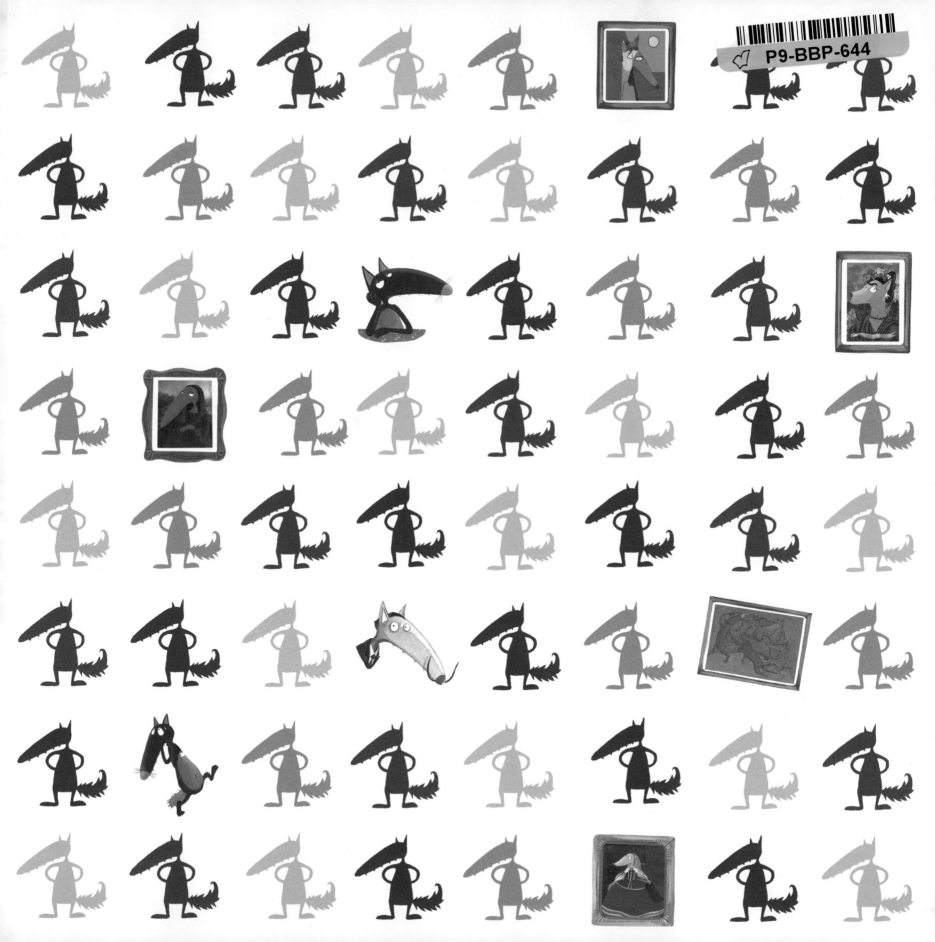

To Matt, who comes with me to museums when I ask him.
OL

*To our little readers: Thank you for making
our Wolf your adventurous friend.*
ET

The Wolf
Who Solved the Mystery of the Missing Mask

By Orianne Lallemand

Illustrations by Éléonore Thuillier

AUZOU

There once was a wolf who didn't like museums.
"Museums are boring," he told everyone.

Wolf was surprised when his friends showed up at his home one morning. "We're taking you to the museum today," Wolfette announced. Wolf frowned, but he didn't want to disappoint her, so he agreed to go along. He liked Wolfette a lot!

Salvador Dawolfi

Managing Director: Gauthier Auzou
Editor: Laura Levy
Assistant Editor: Marjorie Demaria
Layout: Sarah Bouyssou
Production: Lucile Pierret
Project Management for the English Edition: Ariane Laine-Forrest
English Translation: MaryChris Bradley

ISBN: 9782733867402

www.auzou.com
Follow us on Facebook
https://www.facebook.com/auzoupublishing

"Well, I rode on a polar bear's back, met a dodo, escaped from a dangerous dinosaur, solved a mystery and explored a wondrous forest," Wolf told her. "You were right, Wolfette, museums *are* exciting. Let's come back soon!"

Museum

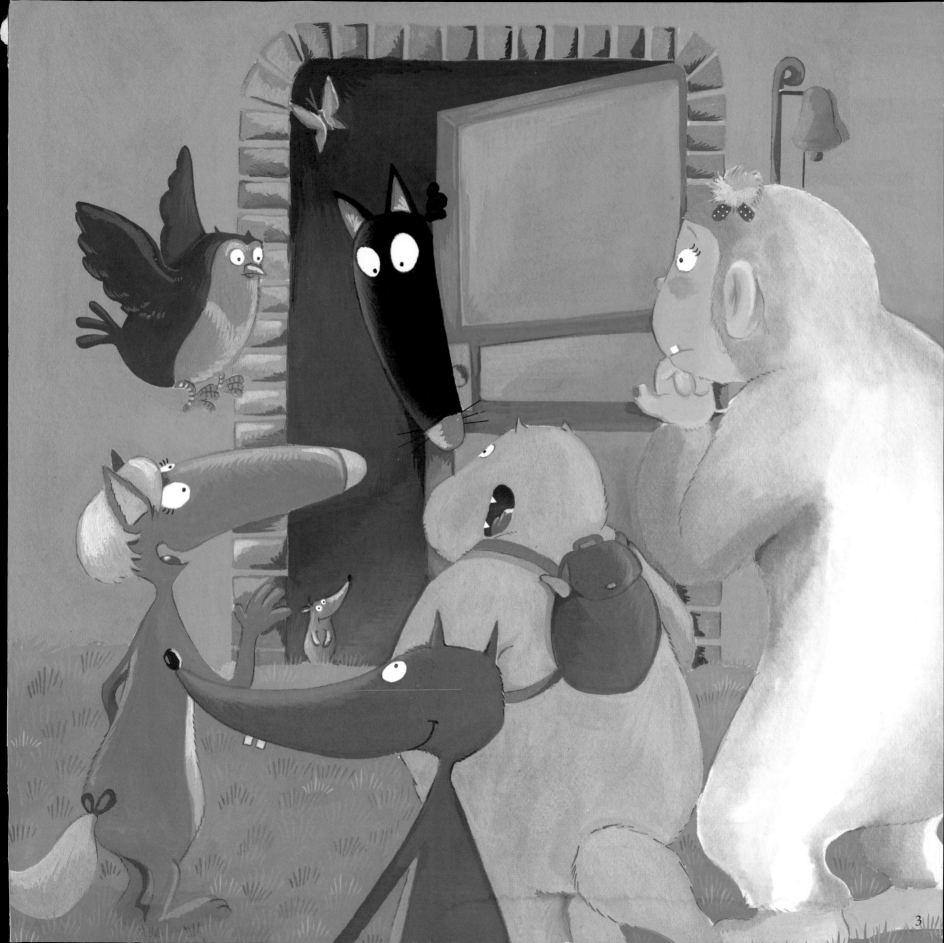

Leonardo da Wolfinci

As soon as they entered the museum, Mr. Owl pointed out one of his favorite paintings. "This piece is by the world-famous, Leonardo da Wolfinci. He painted this in the early 1500s. Not only is the subject beautiful, but her smile is very mysterious."

Veláwolfquez

Wolfmeer

Arcimwolfo

"It's true, she is pretty," sighed Alex,
turning toward Wolf.
But Wolf had already left the room.

5

In the next room, Wolf stood in front of a curious picture. He leaned his head to the left, then to the right, trying to make sense of it. "Is my vision bad or is there something wrong with this painting?" he wondered aloud.

Pablo Wolfcasso

A little rat in a uniform overheard Wolf and started to giggle.

Pablo Wo

Paul Kleewolf

"This portrait was done by Pablo Wolfcasso. By the way, I'm Barnabas, the museum guard. Now, let's go find a painting that you'll enjoy."

Frida Kahwolflo

H. A. Jacquemart

Wolf happily accompanied Barnabas into
the next room. "This is our sculpture
 collection. Some of these pieces are over
a thousand-years-old, others are
barely twenty!"

"Splendid!" exclaimed Wolf, as he climbed
onto a magnificent statue of a polar bear.

"Hey! Off the statue!" scolded Barnabas. "That's a valuable work of art ..."

REEEPPP
REEEPPP
REEEPPP

Venus de Miwolf

Pompon

"Oh no! That's the museum alarm!" a worried Barnabas yelled over the commotion. "I must find out what has happened!"

Wolf tried to keep up with Barnabas, but the museum was a giant maze of rooms! Discouraged, he stopped to look around.

Some guests were painting or drawing. Wolf paused to take a closer look at a snowy landscape that seemed very familiar. "It's the Himalayas!" he thought.

"Thief! Thief!" Barnabas yelled!

Wolf ran into the next room where he found the little museum guard in an awful state!

"Our tribal mask has been stolen! It's a one-of-a-kind! Oh, what a disaster!" cried Barnabas.

"Try to remain calm," said Wolf, glancing around. "The robber can't be far away. Look, footprints!"

Saber-tooth tiger

Dodo

Following the footprints, Wolf and Barnabas entered an enormous room. Wolf stopped in front of an odd-looking bird. "Dodo, what a silly name," he said. "I've never seen a bird like this before."

"That's because they're extinct," explained Barnabas.

Wolf was shocked. Museums were more interesting than he'd thought.

Giant Penguin

Following the footprints toward the next room, Wolf noticed a sinister shadow lurking in the doorway. "Oh, the crook is clearly not in there," he stammered as he backed away.

"That's just a shadow, Wolf! It belongs to a dinosaur skeleton," Barnabas assured him.

The Wooly Mammoth

Mammoth

DINOSAURS

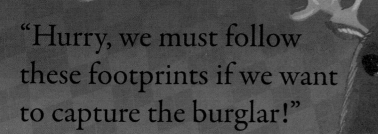

"Hurry, we must follow these footprints if we want to capture the burglar!"

17

Pterodactyl
Egg Fossil

Wolf

Triceratops

Wolf walked quickly, keeping a
cautious eye on the dinosaurs.

18

That's when he spotted something pink on the floor. It was a little bow, covered in pink fur. Wolf frowned. His suspicions had been confirmed!

Lost in thought, he hurried after Barnabas.

Wolf

Lascaux cave paintings

Flints

Wolf

Barnabas was standing near some terracotta pots and primitive tools. "Thanks to these objects, we know how our ancestors lived," he explained. "Holy felony! I just noticed something . . . a flint is missing!"

"The crook must have used it to smash the display case the mask was in," whispered Wolf.

BOOM! "That came from the next room. The thief!" Barnabas shouted.

21

The two friends resumed their chase. Breathless, Barnabas stopped in front of the pharaoh Tutankhamun's sarcophagus. "There's no one here! I don't understand, there's the only one way in or out of this room. It's as if the thief vanished into thin air!"

"Not so fast," replied Wolf, knocking on the sarcophagus lid.

"Not again!" Barnabas was furious. "I told you earlier not to touch the exhibits!" But he stopped dead as the lid of the sarcophagus slowly creaked open . . .

23

. . . revealing, Miss Yeti! And in her arms was the stolen mask.

"I suspected it was you," Wolf sighed. "Come on, Miss Yeti, let's get you out of there."

Miss Yeti burst into tears.
"I-I'm truly sorry," she wailed. "But this mask looks
so-so much like my father.
I just wanted to hug it. I didn't mean to take it,
but when the alarm went off, I ran!"

"Now, now, don't cry," said the little rat. "We will put it back in
its place and no one will ever know it was missing."

As Wolf left the room, his eyes were drawn to a remarkable painting. It looked like his forest, but more beautiful. His heart thumping, he sat down to admire it.

Henri Wolfseau

"There, you see?" Barnabas cried happily, "I told you, love at first sight. Art can capture the heart and move you. It can even transport you to new and wonderful places! At last, a piece of art that you enjoy."

27

Henri Wolftisse

Wolf sat contemplating the painting for a long time. When he finally rejoined his friends, they were standing in front of a picture, still listening to Mr. Owl.

Wolfard Munch

"Ah, there you are, Wolf," grumbled Owl. "I'd hoped you would try to appreciate the museum. But as soon as we arrived, you disappeared."

Museum
Shop

"Where were you all day, Wolf, and whatever were you doing?" Wolfette asked as they exited the museum.